Walt Disney's CLASSIC

101 DALMATIANS

Illustrated by Bill Langley and Ron Dias
Adapted by Justine Korman

A GOLDEN BOOK • NEW YORK
Western Publishing Company, Inc., Racine, Wisconsin 53404

Pongo, Perdita, and their fifteen puppies all lived in a cozy little house on a quiet little street in London. Their humans lived there, too: Roger, who was tall and thin and played the piano; and Anita, who laughed a lot. They all got along splendidly and were very happy.

One day the doorbell rang, and in came Cruella de Vil. The only one in that cozy little house who liked Cruella was Anita, and that was because they had gone to school together.

"I'm so glad the puppies have finally gotten their spots!"
Cruella said, stroking their soft fur. "I'll pay for them now."

"Pay for Lucky?" gasped Anita. "And Patch and Pepper and
Freckles and...and...Oh, Cruella, we couldn't part with them."

"Don't be silly, Anita," snapped Cruella. "You can't possibly
keep fifteen puppies."

Roger put his foot down. "We are not selling them," he said.
"And that's final!"

Cruella was so furious, she rushed out of the house,
slamming the door behind her.

One frosty night a few weeks later, Pongo and Perdita went out for a walk with Roger and Anita. The puppies were at home, asleep in their basket.

Suddenly two men burst into the house. One was tall and thin and ugly. The other was short and fat and also ugly. They put all the puppies into a big satchel. Then they carried the satchel out to their truck and sped away.

After being driven about for what seemed like hours, the fifteen puppies found themselves in a big room filled with scores of other Dalmatian puppies. Lounging on a couch in front of a television set were the two horrid men—the Badun brothers— who had kidnapped them.

The other Dalmatians told them that Jasper and Horace Badun worked for Cruella de Vil, who had bought the puppies from pet stores.

Back at home, Pongo and Perdita were horrified to find their puppies gone.

"It's that evil Cruella de Vil," Perdita said, sobbing. "She has stolen our puppies! Oh, Pongo, do you think we'll ever find them?"

They decided to try the Twilight Bark, a system of long and short barks used by dogs to pass along news. Sometimes only gossip went from dog to dog, but at other times the Twilight Bark carried important information.

Pongo and Perdita convinced Roger to take them on another walk. While they were out, they barked long and loud, until they were certain that all the dogs in London would be on the lookout for their puppies.

That night the Twilight Bark even reached a quiet farm in Sussex where an old sheepdog known as the Colonel lay sleeping.

"Alert, alert!" shouted Sergeant Tibs, a cat who lived on the farm. "Vital message coming in from London."

The Colonel lifted one shaggy ear to listen to the faint message. "Fifteen puppies have been stolen!" he cried.

"I heard puppies barking at the old De Vil mansion," said Tibs. "You don't suppose..."

"We should investigate right away!" the Colonel told Tibs. They headed straight for the gloomy mansion.

Once they arrived, the Colonel braced himself against a wall as Tibs climbed up onto his shoulder to peek through a window.

"Lucky?" Tibs called. "Freckles? Are you there?" Then he saw all the puppies. "Good night!" said the cat. "There are a whole lot of you. I'm looking for fifteen puppies who were stolen from London."

"I was stolen!" Lucky spoke out. "And so were my brothers and sisters."

The Baduns heard the noise and headed for the window to investigate. Tibs went away, but only after promising to bring back help and to tell the puppies' parents where they were.

Next morning, just after the Baduns had switched on the television set, Cruella de Vil arrived in her fancy roadster.

"It's got to be done today!" cried Cruella.

"But you couldn't get a dozen coats out of the whole caboodle," protested Jasper, pointing to the puppies.

"Then I'll have to settle for half a dozen," said Cruella. "Just do it!"

She dashed out. Moments later they heard her car roar away.

Horace and Jasper turned back to their television program.

Sergeant Tibs had returned just in time to hear Cruella give the order. "You kids better get out of here right now before they make coats out of you," he whispered. Then he shoved one of the puppies toward a hole in the wall.

"It's too small," protested the pup.

"Squeeze!" ordered Tibs.

Squeeze the puppy did, and he got through. One by one, the other puppies followed. Each time one got through, plaster crumbled and the hole got a little larger.

Suddenly the two thugs realized that the puppies were escaping. The chase was on! Tibs and the puppies scooted through the dark and twisting halls of the mansion. Soon they found themselves trapped at a dead end. The thugs raised their clubs to strike.

At that moment Pongo and Perdita crashed through the window with a blast of glass and freezing air. The angry Dalmatian parents fought off the astonished thugs as all the puppies scampered to safety.

Once all the dogs were safely outside, they hastily thanked
the Colonel and Sergeant Tibs and bade them farewell. Then
they hurried toward London. Pongo and Perdita led the way,
their fifteen puppies and the scores of other Dalmatian pups
right behind them.

When they reached a frozen stream, they delicately crossed
the slippery surface. This way they wouldn't leave paw prints
behind them. Then they resumed the race home.

All along the route, the Dalmatians were helped by other dogs who had heard about their escape. A black Labrador retriever arranged for them to ride to London in the back of a moving van which was being repaired. The Dalmatians waited in a shed while the van was being fixed.

Suddenly Cruella's big car came up the street. Despite the ice, she had followed their tracks all the way to the shed. She parked her car outside and waited.

"Oh, Pongo," said Perdita. "How will we get to the van?"

Pongo noticed that there were a lot of ashes in the fireplace. If they all rolled in the soot, they would look just like black Labradors. And that's exactly what they did.

When the van was ready to leave, the dogs marched calmly out of the shed. They passed Cruella's car and made it to the back of the van.

One after another, the soot-covered puppies were lifted into the van. At last only a few puppies remained on the street. As Pongo bent to pick one up, a tiny avalanche of snow fell from the roof and buried another puppy.

The puppy quickly shook himself off, but the snow had washed away the soot. From her car, Cruella could see the white fur and black spots.

"They're escaping!" shouted Cruella as the van moved away.

Cruella's car sputtered, then roared. Snow spun from its wheels.

Faster and faster went the van. But Cruella drew closer and closer. She drove so close to the van that the dogs could see her face. She was screaming in anger. Then she began to scream in fear. There was a cliff ahead and only room enough for the van to pass. Cruella tried to stop her car, but it spun sideways on the ice and slid into a ditch. The last the Dalmatians saw of Cruella, she was standing beside her wrecked car having a nasty temper tantrum.

Pongo laughed, and all the puppies cheered. When the van reached London, the Dalmatians jumped out and ran straight to that cozy little house on that quiet little street. Roger and Anita were overjoyed to see each and every one of them. And when they counted the dogs, they discovered that they now had 101 Dalmatians. They realized that some changes would have to be made.

"We'll buy a big house in the country," said Roger. "We'll have a Dalmatian plantation!"

And so they did exactly that. And Pongo and Perdita and all the spotted puppies lived there happily ever after.